for Clara & Kenneth
A.K.A
Mama & Papa Sneed

MANY SHAPES of CLAY

Written & illustrated By Kenesha Sneed

PRESTEL
Munich · London · New York

This is Eisha (you say it like “Eee-sha”).

And this is her cat who loves to take long naps.

This is Eisha's Mama.

She works in a small studio inside the basement of their apartment where she makes shapes from clay.

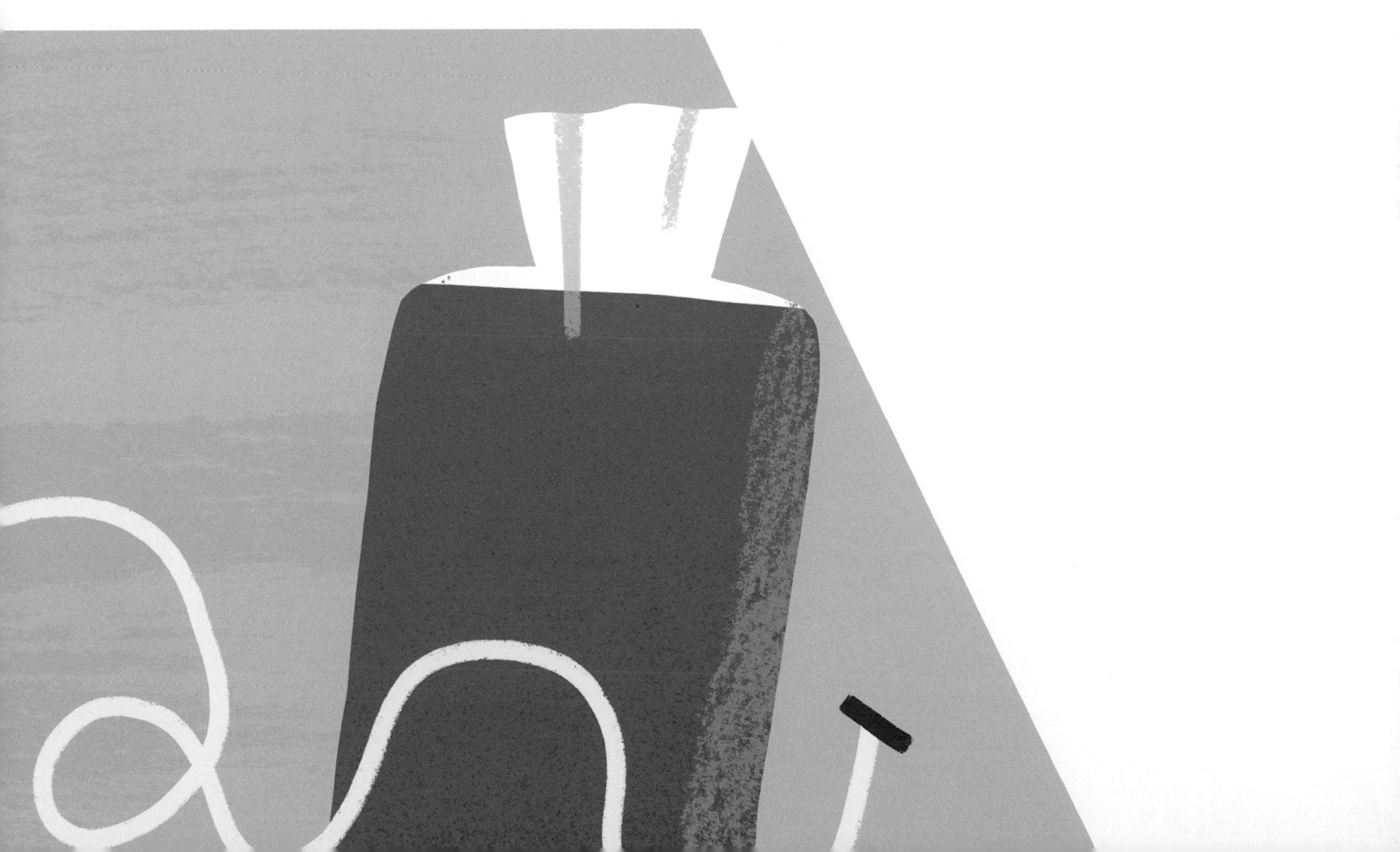

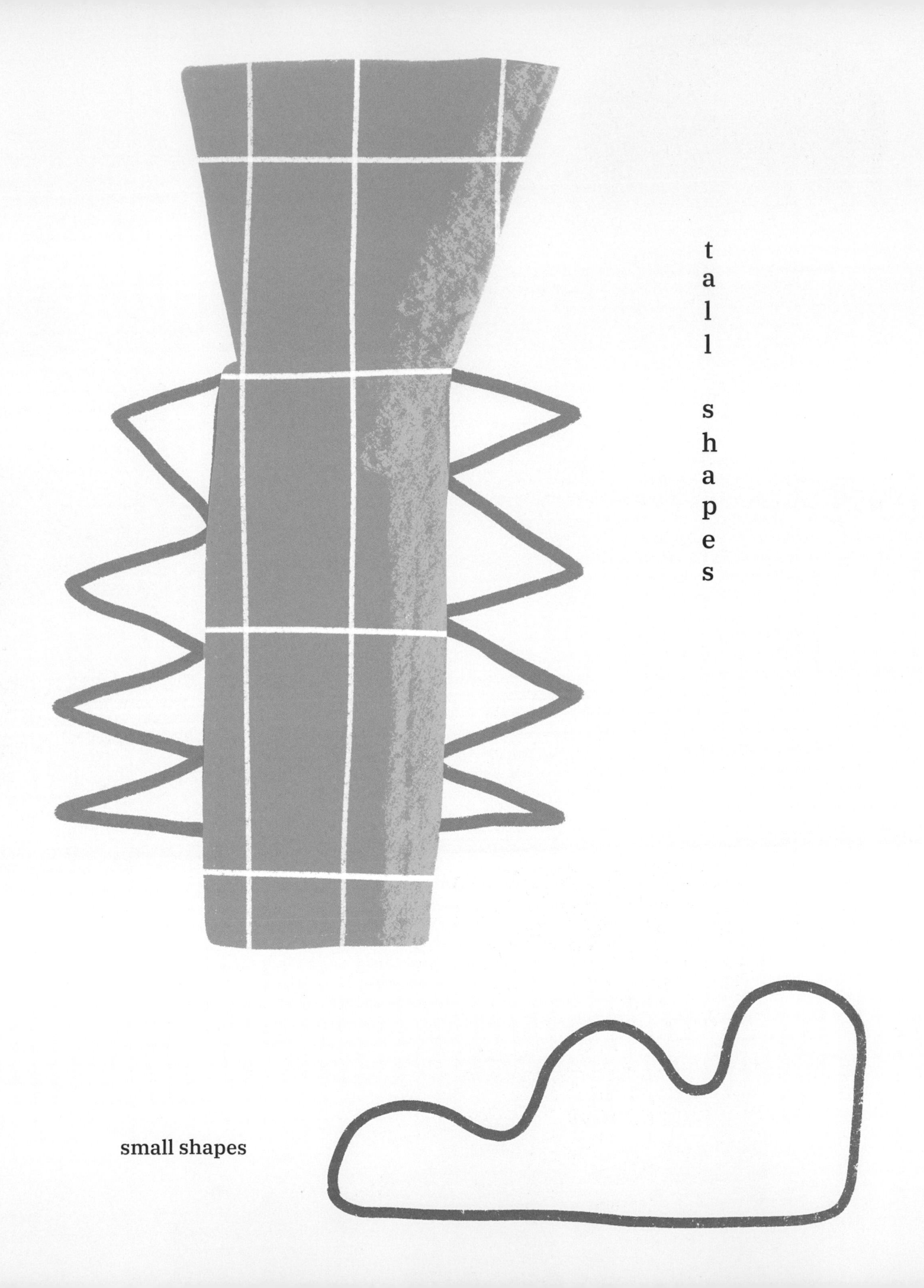
tall shapes
small shapes

even bumpy colorful shapes

Eisha asks her mama why she doesn't play with the shapes.

"Why do you leave them on the shelves?"

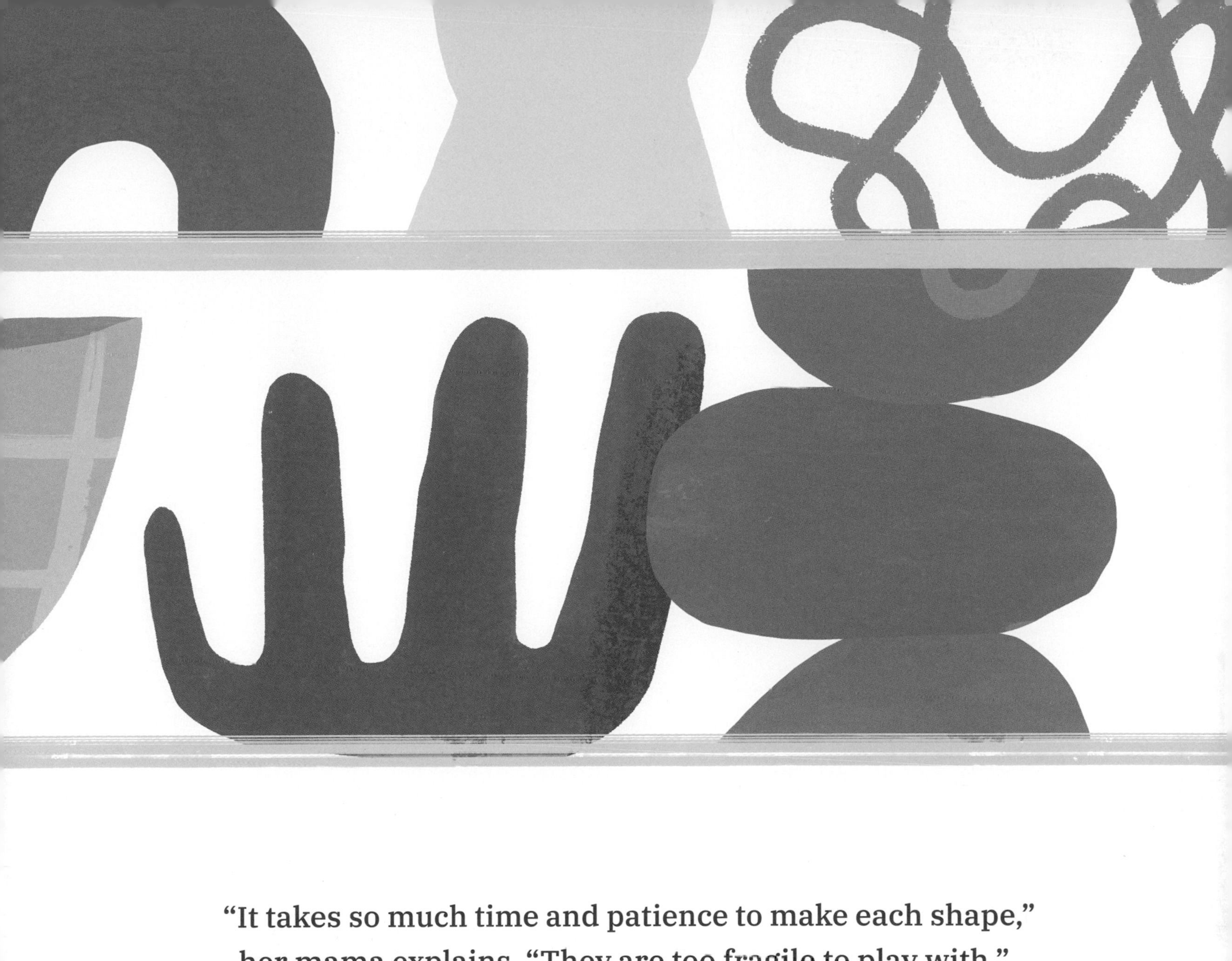

"It takes so much time and patience to make each shape," her mama explains. "They are too fragile to play with."

Mama slices off a chunk of clay like butter, then rolls it into a ball like dough and hands it to Eisha.

Eisha stretches and smoothes and rolls the cool clay in her hands. She doesn't know what she'll make today.

"Maybe I'll make a two-headed lizard with polka dots," she thinks to herself.

One shape in particular makes
Eisha very happy.

It reminds her of the day last summer when
she and Papa picked a handful of lemons.
She paints her shape the same bright yellow.

“All this hard work deserves a pause,” Mama says. “How about some fresh air?”

Sweat drips down from the top of her head to the tip of her chin. Mama misses Papa too.

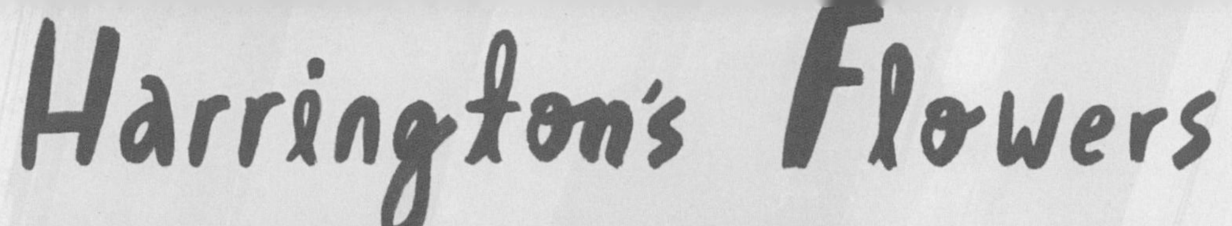

Outside, a summer breeze rustles through the neighborhood trees while the sun slowly sinks behind the buildings.

Eisha sits on the stoop and
plays with her yellow shape.

The whole neighborhood seems to be taking a pause.

Except for Ms. Harrington from the flower market.
She rides past with a backpack full of lavender.

She waves at Eisha as a sprig of lavender falls out
of her backpack and floats down to the sidewalk.

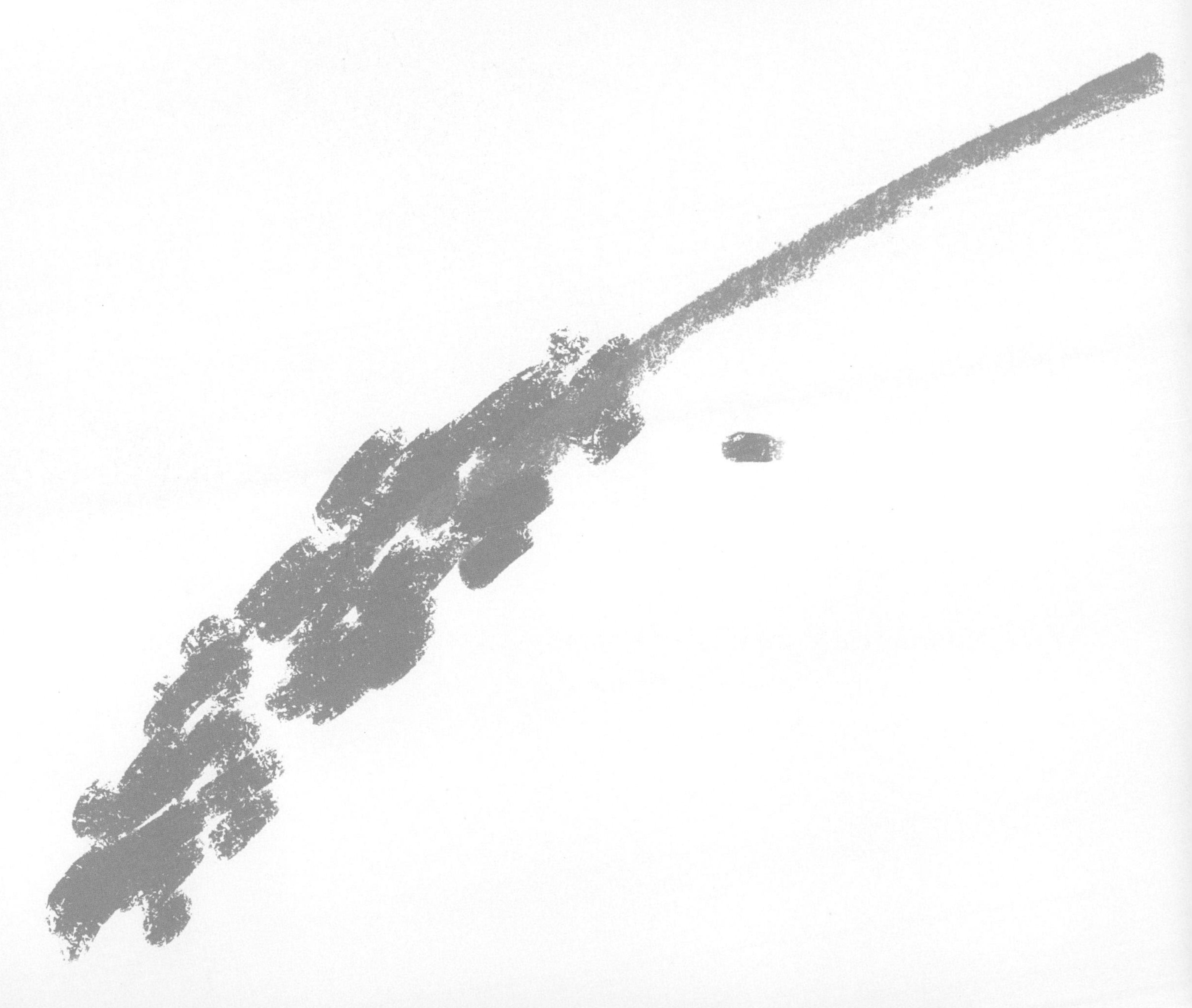

Eisha wonders if Miss Harrington will notice the missing sprig when she gets home. And if she does, will she feel sad about it?

As Eisha sits on the stoop, she imagines so many things she could do with her shape.

“Maybe we’ll go to the beach someday,” Eisha says to herself.

The sound of the ocean hugging the shore
as water cooled her toes would feel so good.

The rumble of a skateboard interrupts Eisha's daydream. She looks down at her shape. It's less yellow now, like the color of a lemon that's lost its taste, and not as soft.

But that’s OK, because now it makes music when
Eisha taps it with her fingers!

Tap, tap, tap . . . Eisha taps her clay.

Tap, tap . . .

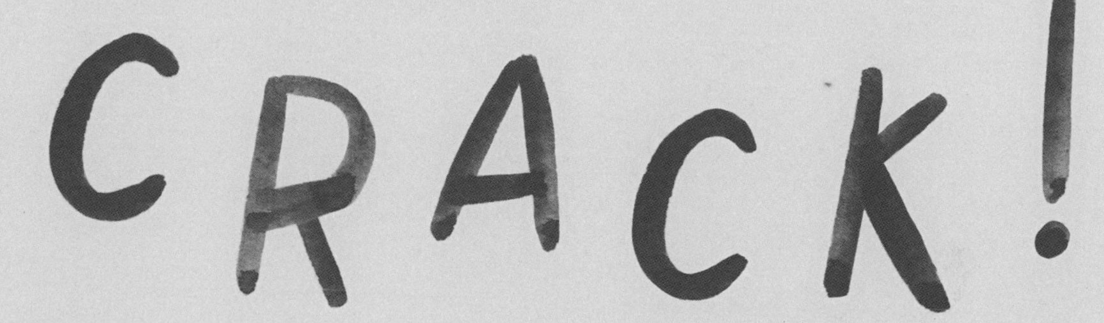

Eisha's shape has broken into many shapes on the ground. Each piece reflects the sadness she feels.

Eisha tries to think of ways to put the pieces back together.

Tape wouldn't last very long . . .

. . . and glue always sticks to the wrong things.

What Eisha feels is hard to describe—like something that is too heavy to lift. Like something that might last forever.

The sunlight is fading and the breeze
has stopped blowing through the trees.

Eisha's eyes fill with tears as she looks down at all the broken pieces. "What happened?" asks Mama, as she scoops Eisha up onto her lap.

"I gave my shape so much time and patience, but now it's in pieces." Eisha says.

"It's OK to feel sad about those broken pieces," Mama says. "There are times—many times—when we lose the things we love."

Mama somehow knows what Eisha is feeling. I never knew she could feel the same feelings, Eisha thinks, and hugs her Mama close.

Together they pick up the broken pieces and walk past the shapes on Mama’s shelves, stepping over the last step where the cat purrs sound asleep.

“You can’t always fix what’s broken, but you can always try,” Mama says as she pulls out a small box from under her bed.

Inside are spindles of twine in different sizes, colors, and textures.

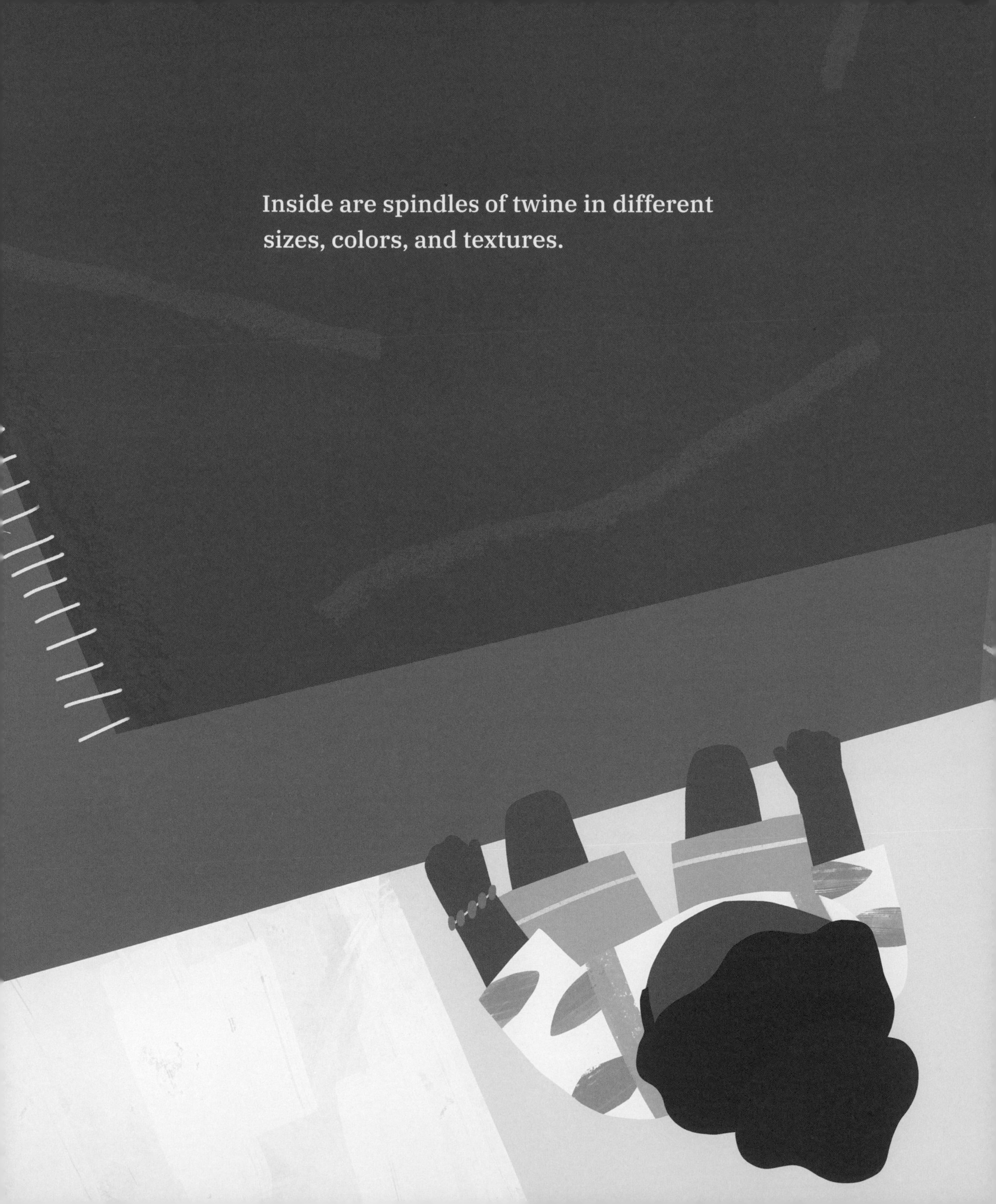

Slowly, with patience and care, Mama and Eisha connect all the broken pieces together by looping twine around each one.

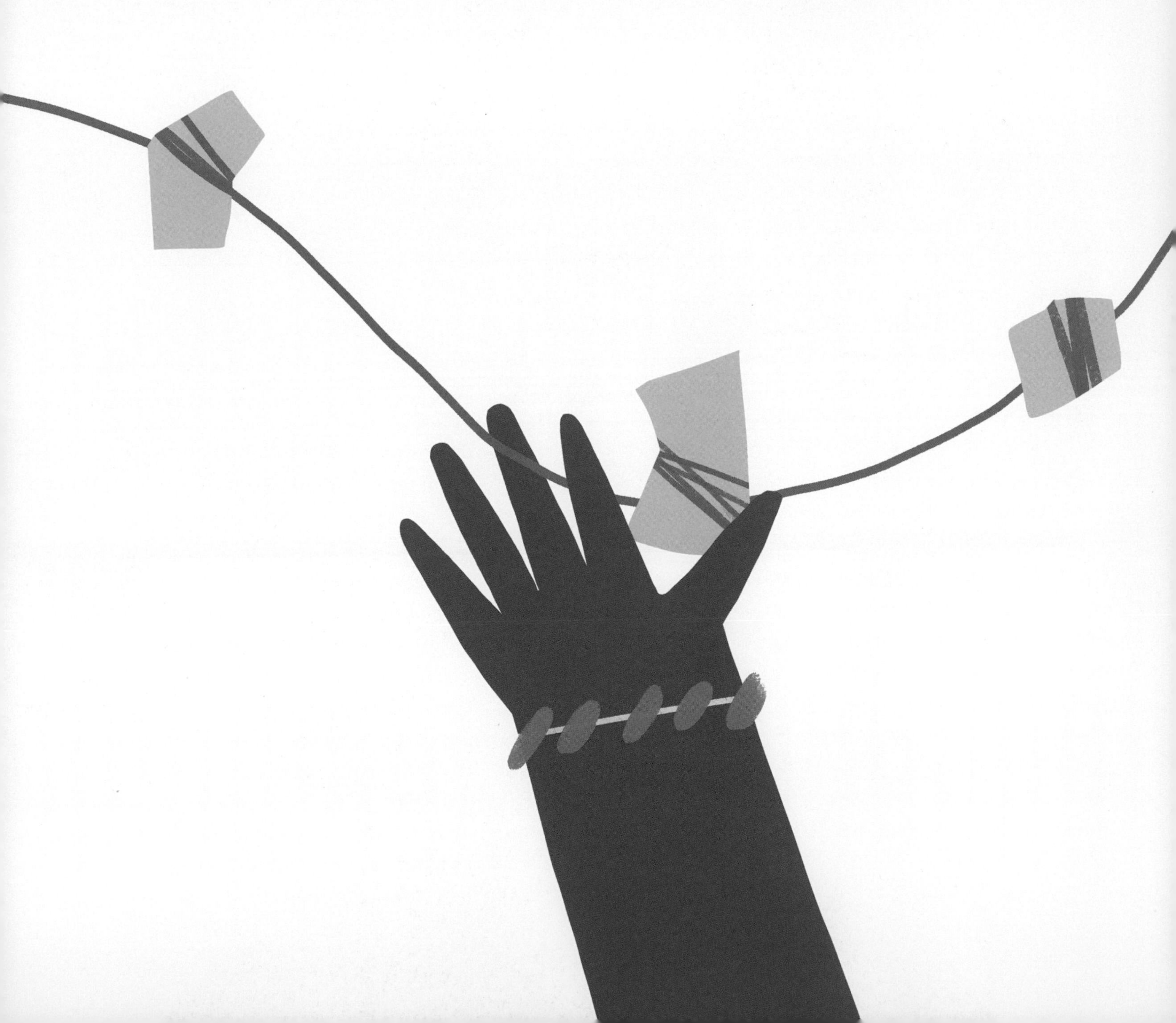

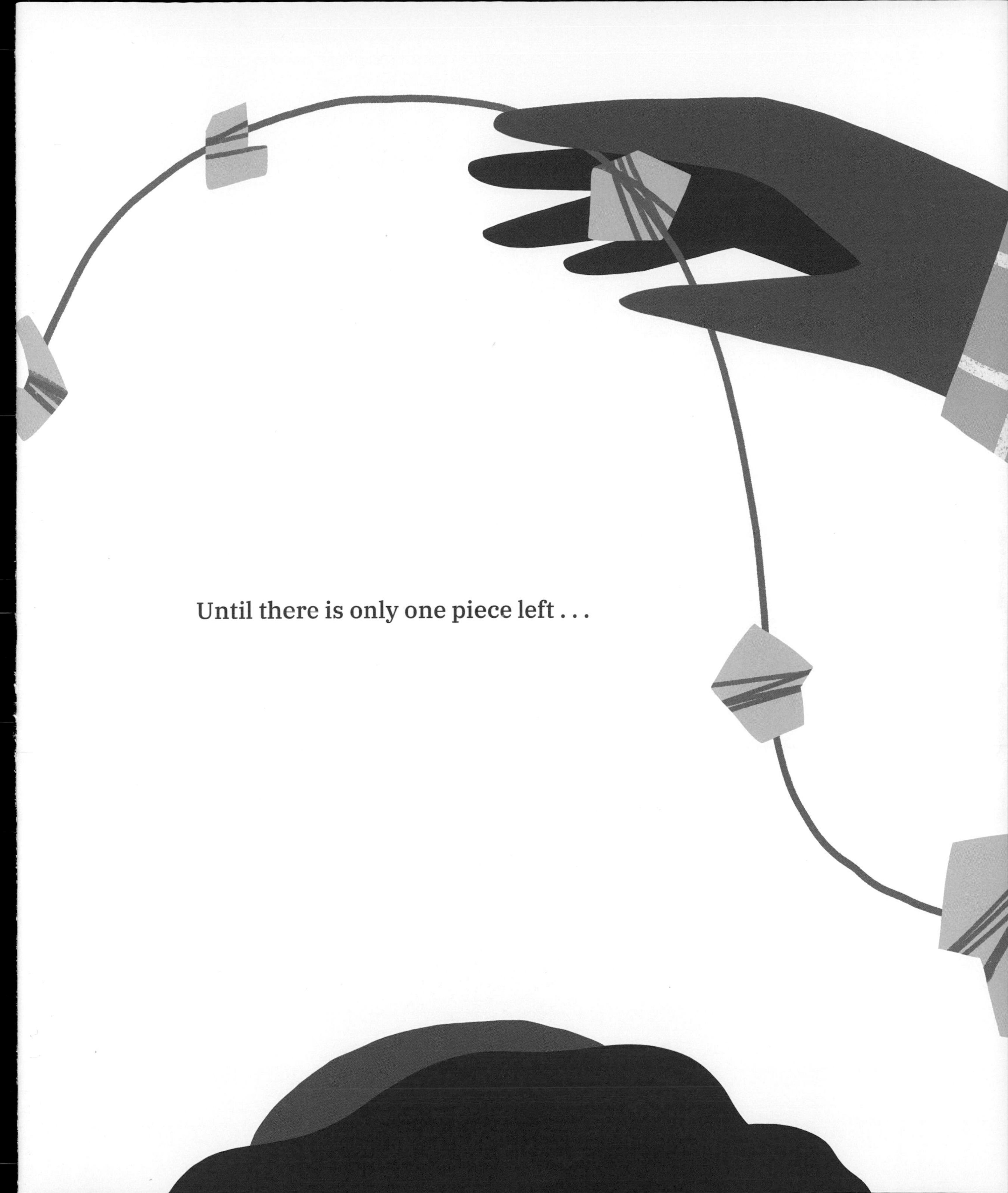

Until there is only one piece left . . .

"Maybe I can make it into
something new tomorrow?"
Eisha thinks out loud.

“What a wonderful idea,” Mama says, gazing at Eisha with a warm smile. “Now let’s wash up and see what we can come up with for dinner.”

Prestel Verlag, Munich · London · New York 2021
A member of Penguin Random House Verlagsgruppe GmbH
Neumarkter Strasse 28 · 81673 Munich

Library of Congress Cataloging-in-Publication Data

Names: Sneed, Kenesha, author, artist.
Title: Many shapes of clay / Kenesha Sneed.
Description: Munich ; New York, NY : Prestel Verlag, 2021. |
Audience: Ages 5-8 | Audience: Grades K-1
Identifiers: LCCN 2020010819 | ISBN 9783791374680 (hardcover)
Subjects: LCSH: Grief in children--Juvenile literature. | Parent and
child--Juvenile literature. | Ceramic sculpture--Juvenile literature.
Classification: LCC BF723.G75 S66 2021 | DDC 155.9/37083--dc23
LC record available at https://lccn.loc.gov/2020010819

A CIP catalogue record for this book is available from the British Library.

Editorial direction: Holly La Due
Design and layout: Anjali Pala
Production management: Susanne Hermann

Prestel Publishing compensates the CO_2 emissions produced from
the making of this book by supporting a reforestation project in Brazil.
Find further information on the project here:
www.ClimatePartner.com/14044-1912-1001

Penguin Random House Verlagsgruppe FSC® N001967
Printed on the FSC®-certified paper
Printed in Slovenia

ISBN 978-3-7913-7468-0

www.prestel.com